Tom and Ricky
and the
Garage Sale Mystery

Bob Wright

High Noon Books
Novato, California

Cover Design: Nancy Peach
Interior Illustrations: Herb Heidinger
Story: Miriam Ylvisaker

Glossary: clothes, tools, drawers, metal

International Standard Book Number: 0-87879-394-1

10 09 08 07 06 05 04 03
15 14 13 12 11 10 9 8 7

You'll enjoy all the High Noon Books.
Write for a free full list of titles.

Contents

CHAPTER 1

Making Plans

Ricky got on his bike. Patches, his dog, was right in back of him. He started off for Tom's house.

"Where are you going?" Ricky's mother called.

"I'll be at Tom's house. We're going over to the creek to fish," Ricky called back.

"What about your pole?" she called.

Ricky turned back. "That's right. I forgot."

Ricky ran into the garage. He got his fishing pole. Then he started again for Tom's house.

Ricky stopped his bike in front of Tom's house. "Tom! Tom!" he called.

Tom came out of the garage.

"Are you ready?" Ricky asked.

"Ready? For what?" Tom asked.

"I guess you forgot. We were going to go fishing," Ricky said.

"That's right. I forgot all about it. I told my mom I'd help her. We're cleaning out the garage," Tom said.

"Do you have much more to do?" Ricky asked.

"A lot," Tom said.

"Well, let me help. Then we can still get to the creek early," Ricky said.

"OK. Come on. Let's get going," Tom said.

Ricky started to help Tom. Patches sat and watched. There was a lot of work to do.

"We haven't cleaned the garage for a long time. There are a lot of things here," Tom said.

Ricky looked at everything. "There sure are," he said.

Then Tom's mother came into the garage. "Hello, Ricky. Thanks for helping," she said.

"I wanted to help Tom. That way we can still get over to the creek. It will go faster with two of us," Ricky said.

Tom's mother looked around the garage. "You know what? I think this is a good time to stop," she said.

"Why is that?" Tom asked.

"I need to look at these things. Why don't you go fishing now? We can start again when you come back," she answered.

"Oh, boy! Come on, Tom," Ricky said.

Patches sat up. He was ready to go.

Tom got his pole. The two boys and Patches started out for the creek.

"Which way do you want to go?" Tom asked.

"Let's go up to Front Street. It's faster that way," Ricky answered.

"This is a good morning to fish," Tom said.

"I bet some other people might be there," Ricky said.

The boys got to the creek. They put their bikes next to a tree. Then they locked them.

"Look! We're the only ones here," Tom said.

"We're lucky. Come on. Get your pole," Ricky said.

The two boys went over to the creek.

"Here's a good place," Ricky said. They sat next to the creek. Then they put their lines into the water. Patches sat down near them.

"What if we catch a lot of fish today?" Tom asked.

"We could sell them," Ricky answered.

"It would be nice to make some money," Tom said.

"You're right. I'd like to buy a new fishing pole," Ricky said.

"Me, too," Tom said.

"Well, the fish better start biting," Ricky said.

Tom and Ricky sat by the creek for a long time. But there weren't any bites on their lines.

"Tom, I just don't think this is a good morning for fishing," Ricky said.

"There go our new fishing lines," Tom said.

"That's right. No fish, no money," Ricky said.

"Wait! We could sell things from my garage," Tom said.

"We could have a garage sale," Ricky said.

"What's a garage sale?" Tom asked.

"That's when you sell things you don't need any more. I bet we have a lot of things at my house, too," Ricky answered.

"Come on. It's a good idea. Let's get going," Tom said.

"Here, Patches," Ricky called. Patches came running out from the trees. Then the boys rode back home.

CHAPTER 2

Finding Things

Tom and Ricky got back to Tom's house. They ran inside.

"What's up, boys? How many fish did you get?" Tom's mother asked.

"Not one. They weren't biting," Tom said.

"You weren't there very long," she said.

"We had a better idea," Tom said.

"What's that?" she asked.

"We're going to have a garage sale," Tom said.

"You have to have a lot of things for a garage sale. Where are you going to get them?" she asked.

"What about the things in our garage?" Tom asked.

"A lot of that is no good. But I think you could sell some of it," she said.

"We have some things in our garage. I know my dad wants to get rid of a lot of it," Ricky said.

"Where are you going to have the garage sale?" she asked.

"Can we have it here?" Tom asked.

"I think you can have it here. But don't wait too long. I need that garage all cleaned up," Tom's mother said.

"What about next Saturday?" Tom asked.

"That will be OK. A one day sale is a good idea," she said.

"You will need a lot of things for a garage sale. We have some. Ricky has some. But that isn't enough. Where will you get the rest?" she asked.

"We can go up this street. We'll ask people to give us old things they don't want," Tom said.

"I can do the same thing on my street," Ricky said.

"How will you let people know about the garage sale?" she asked.

"That's right, Ricky. How will we do that?" Tom asked.

"We can make some notes. Then we can leave them with people. We can even put them on cars," Ricky said.

"Come on. Let's start now," Tom said.

"Where shall we go first?" Ricky asked.

"Wait. How are we going to carry things back here?" Tom asked.

"Let's get two boxes. We can each take one," Ricky said.

"What about the notes?" Tom said.

"That's right. Let's do those first. We have to get them done," Ricky said.

Tom got some paper and pencils. The boys sat down and made notes to give out.

The notes said:

```
Garage Sale — Saturday

9 - 12

818 Rock Street
```

They made a lot of them. Then they started out.

People had more things than the boys thought. They got old dishes, old toys, old clothes, and old tables. Everything was old. A lot of it was broken. They brought everything back to Tom's garage.

Tom's mother went out to the garage. She looked at all the things. "No more, boys. That's it. I thought I was cleaning this garage. Now it's full again," she said.

Tom and Ricky looked at everything. "We do have a lot," Tom said.

"We sure do," Ricky said.

*"No more, boys. That's it.
I thought I was cleaning this garage," she said.*

"I hope you boys sell everything. I don't want anything left over after the sale," she said.

"We just have one more place to go," Tom said.

"Oh, no. Not more things," Tom's mother said.

"Mr. Bell saw us getting things. He said he has some things he wants to give us," Tom said.

"Mr. Bell is our good friend. But that's the last one," she said.

"Mr. Bell has a big, old home. I bet he has a lot of old things," Ricky said.

"Don't take too many things. We already have a lot in here," she said.

"We won't," Tom said.

The boys started down the street to Mr. Bell's house. Mr. Bell was old. He had lived in the same house all his life.

"Hello, boys," Mr. Bell said.

"We're here to get some things for our garage sale," Tom said.

"I gave away a lot of things a year ago. But here. I have some dishes and this wood box," he said.

"That's a funny looking box. It sure has a lot of drawers. What's it for?" Tom asked.

"I don't know. It was my father's. I don't use it. I hope you can sell it," Mr. Bell said.

The boys thanked Mr. Bell. Then they started back for Tom's house.

CHAPTER 3

The Strange Man

The next day the boys got up early. They met in Tom's garage. They needed to get things ready for the sale.

"We sure have a lot of good things," Tom said.

"You're not kidding. Everybody gave us something," Ricky said.

They started to move things around. Then they saw a woman coming over to the garage.

"Who is that?" Tom asked.

"It's Mrs. Rose. You know her. She owns the gift store," Ricky said.

"Good morning, boys. I hear you are going to have a garage sale," Mrs. Rose said.

"Yes, we are getting ready for it now. It will be on Saturday," Tom said.

"I brought some things you might like to sell. Here are some old tools and a few books," Mrs. Rose said.

"Thank you very much," Ricky said.

"We know people will like to buy tools and books," Tom said.

"Have you gotten lots of nice things?" Mrs. Rose asked.

"Yes, we have," Ricky said.

"Look at this old box. Isn't it something?" Tom asked.

"Yes, it sure is. It is made of very pretty wood. And look at all those little drawers," Mrs. Rose said.

"We got it from Mr. Bell," Tom said.

"He said it had been in his house for a long, long time. So it must be very old," Ricky said.

"I really would like to buy that box. I will make sure I get here early for your garage sale," Mrs. Rose said.

"We will see you Saturday," Tom said.

The boys had a lot of work to do. They had to think about how much money they could ask people to pay for each thing.

"This is taking a long time," Ricky said.

"We are almost done," Tom said.

The boys were working hard.

*"I really would like to buy that box,"
Mrs. Rose said.*

They did not see a man coming. The man looked around and then came into the garage.

"What are you boys up to?" the man asked.

"We are getting ready for a garage sale," Ricky said.

"Where did you get all these old things?" the man asked.

"People gave them to us. We're going to sell them," Tom said.

"I am looking for something. You had better let me look around," the man said.

The man looked mad. The boys did not know what to do.

"Where did you get this box?" the man asked. It was the box Mr. Bell had given them.

He picked it up. He looked at it. He turned it up and down. He opened and closed the drawers.

"I asked where you got this box," the man said.

"From an old house near here," Tom said.

"I want this box. I want you to sell it to me right now. How much do you want for it?" the man asked.

"The sale is not until Saturday," Tom said.

Now the man looked very mad. He held on hard to the box. At last he put it down.

"OK, if that is the way you want it. But you better not sell that box to anyone else," the man said. He walked away.

"How about that," Tom said.

"What will we do? Mrs. Rose wants to buy that box," Ricky said.

"I know. I don't like any of this," Ricky said.

"I think we had better tell Sergeant Collins about all this," Tom said.

"Yes, and on Saturday we will have to watch for that man," Ricky said.

CHAPTER 4

Garage Sale Day

On Saturday, the boys were up early. They met at Tom's house. Everything in the garage had a little tag on it. They put all the things on tables.

"Do you think anyone will come?" Ricky asked.

"I think so. We know two people will come anyway. Mrs. Rose and that man," Tom said.

Ricky laughed. "I don't know about that man. I don't think I want to see him again," he said.

"I hope we make some money," Tom said.

"I do, too. I would really like that new fishing pole," Ricky said.

"Here comes someone," Tom said.

"It's Mr. West from the video store," Ricky said.

"Good morning, boys. How is it going?" Mr. West asked.

"You are the first one here," Ricky said.

"You can have your pick of all the things," Tom said.

Mr. West looked around.

"These are some great tools," he said.

"They came from Mrs. Rose's house," Ricky said.

"Then I know they are good tools. I would like to buy them," Mr. West said.

"And we are glad to sell them," Tom said.

They did not see him pick up something from one of the tables.

Now people were coming fast. Tom and Ricky were very busy. They did not see the man come down into the garage. They did not see him pick up something from one of the tables.

Then Mrs. Rose walked in. "Good morning, boys. It looks like the sale is going well," she said.

"Yes, it is. We are selling everything," Tom said.

"I came to buy that nice box," Rose said.

"It is right here," Ricky said.

He went to the table where they had put the box. It was not there. Then he saw that man walking away down the street. He was going very fast. He was almost running.

"There goes our box," Tom said.

"I bet you are right," Ricky said.

"I am really mad," Tom said.

"That man is no good," Ricky said.

"Mrs. Rose, we're very sorry. It looks like that man came here to take that box," Tom said.

"Why would he do such a thing?" Mrs. Rose asked.

"We don't know. But we will try to find out," Ricky said.

"And we will try to get the box back for you," Tom said.

CHAPTER 5

Going to the Dump

At last people started to leave. The garage sale was over. It was noon. The boys looked around.

"We really sold a lot of things," Tom said.

"We sure did. Now we have to get things cleaned up. There isn't much left. It won't take long," Ricky said.

The boys filled up the boxes. Then they cleaned up the garage.

Tom's dad walked in. "There isn't much left," he said.

"No, not much," Tom said.

"You boys can help me get those boxes in the car. We'll take all of it down to the dump," Tom's dad said.

Tom's mother said, "That's a very good idea. Now I'll have a clean garage again."

The boys put all the boxes in the car. Then they got in.

Tom's dad asked, "How much did you make?"

"It looks like we did OK," Tom said.

"And we made enough to buy new poles," Ricky said.

"You boys will have to give me two dollars," Tom's dad said.

"What for?" Tom asked.

"We have to pay to dump those boxes," he answered.

The dump was out past the creek. They drove out to it on Front Street. As they passed the creek, Ricky yelled, "Look, Tom! There's that man. The one who took the nice box!"

"Stop the car, Dad," Tom yelled.

"What are you boys going to do?" he asked.

"We're going to get that box back. Mrs. Rose said she wanted to buy it. And anyway, he didn't pay for it," Tom said.

"OK. I'll go to the dump by myself. I'll meet you boys back here by the creek," Tom's dad said.

Tom, Ricky, and Patches jumped out of the car. They didn't see the man anywhere. But they knew he was somewhere near the creek.

The boys ran down into the trees by the creek.

All of a sudden Ricky stopped. "Wait. I hear something over there," he said.

"It could be Patches," Tom said.

"I am going to take a look," Ricky said.

"OK. Be careful," Tom said.

Ricky went down a little way. "Come here," he called to Tom.

Patches was sitting very still under a tree. There was a man walking under the trees. Patches was watching the man.

"Look! There he is," Ricky said.

"What is he doing?" Tom asked.

They watched the man move around.

"He is reading something," Tom said.

"Look at what he has in his hand," Ricky said.

"He has our box," Tom said.

"But what is he doing with it?" Ricky asked.

The man was opening and closing the drawers. He was turning the box over to look at the back.

"He is reading something," Tom said.

The man had a little paper in his hand. He walked over to a tree. Then he turned around and walked back again.

"It looks like he is talking to himself," Ricky said.

"I think he is seeing how many steps it is. He is going from the tree to the creek," Tom said.

The man looked down and moved his feet. Then he bent down to push the grass around with his hands.

"He's looking for something," Tom said.

"Maybe that paper has something on it," Ricky said.

"Maybe it is helping him find what he wants," Tom said.

But the man did not seem to be finding anything. He looked mad.

"He is hiding the box," Ricky said.

The man put the box under some grass by a tree. Then he walked away.

"Look! He dropped the paper," Ricky said.

"I'll get it," Tom said.

CHAPTER 6

A Metal Box

Tom found the paper under some grass. He picked it up and opened it.

"Look, Ricky. See all these lines and numbers. What do you think they mean?" Tom asked.

"It looks like this could be a map," Ricky said.

"Hey, I bet it is," Tom said.

"See, here is a tree. These lines look like they might be water," Ricky said.

"And these lines and this circle might be telling someone where to go," Tom said.

"Or maybe how to find something," Ricky said.

"Look at where this tree is on the paper. Now look at the lines. You know what I think?" Tom asked.

"I sure do," Ricky said.

"Look at that tree down there. Now look at the creek. I think this is a map of where we are right now," Tom said.

"I bet you are right! And that man must have been looking for something right here," Ricky said.

"What's he up to?" Tom asked.

"Maybe we can get the answer from the map," Ricky said.

The boys sat down under a tree.

"This mark must be that tree. What do you think this X means?" Tom asked.

"I don't know. Have you got any idea?" Ricky said.

"It might tell us where to look next," Tom said.

"Hey, you know what? I think that mark is where that old tree used to be," Ricky said.

"You mean that tree the wind blew down last year?" Tom asked.

"Sure. The map was telling him to look for something that is gone," Ricky said.

"Let's look around ourselves," Tom said.

The boys walked over to the first tree. Then they went down to the creek. They kept looking at the map. They ended up at a big circle.

"The circle must be that big bush," Tom said. He put his hand down under it.

"I see something under that bush. It looks like a metal box. Can you get it?" Ricky asked.

"I think I can," Tom said. He pulled it out from under the bush. Then he pulled it open.

"Look. It only has a lot of old yellow papers in it," Tom said.

"My, my. What have you boys found this time?" The man had come back.

CHAPTER 7

The Mystery Ends

Tom and Ricky looked up at the man. They didn't know what to do.

"Those are my papers. I will take them now," the man said.

All of a sudden Tom's father and Sergeant Collins walked out of the trees. "What's going on here?" the Sergeant asked.

"How did you know where we were?" Ricky asked.

Tom's dad looked at Sergeant Collins.

"Tom's dad waited for you. He knew you were after this man. He called me when you didn't meet him," the Sergeant said.

"We knew you would be near the creek. We just kept on looking," Tom's dad said.

The man turned to Sergeant Collins. "I am glad you are here," he said.

"Can you tell me what this is all about?" the Sergeant said.

"He's the man who took the box at the garage sale," Ricky said.

"Wait. I will tell you everything," the man said.

"Go ahead. We're waiting," the Sergeant said.

"I owe these boys a lot. They have helped me very much," the man said. The man didn't look mad.

"Go on," the Sergeant said.

"My father built the house Mr. Bell lives in. That was a long, long time ago. My father told me he hid a box, just like this one, in the house. He told me the box had a map," the man said.

Then Ricky said, "And the map was to this metal box?"

"That's right. In the metal box is this paper. It is very old. But it shows that my father owned a silver mine in Alaska," the man said.

Sergeant Collins looked at the old yellow paper. "It's hard to read. But he is right."

"But why didn't you tell us?" Ricky asked.

"I wasn't sure myself. My father was very old when he told me all this. I had to find out for myself," the man said.

"Can we have the wood box?" Tom asked.

"Yes, you can. But I would like it to go to that nice lady who wanted it," the man said.

"That's what we wanted to do with it," Ricky said.

"What will you do now?" Tom asked.

"I am going to go to Alaska. If I find that mine, I will let you know. If it has silver, I want you both to come and see me. I will pay for your trip," the man said.

"That would be fun," Tom said.

"But wait. Here is $10 for the box I took.

I should not have taken it," the man said.

"Oh, boy. More money," Tom yelled.

"But wait. Here is $10 for the box I took."

"Well, boys. Before you take a trip, we have a little more cleaning to do in the garage," Tom's dad said.

"Come on, Ricky. We'll do that. Then we'll buy our new fishing poles," Tom said.

"Then we'll be ready for Alaska," Ricky said.